TEMPTED

TEMPTED

Just a Taste #1

AYLA COX

TEMPTED
Copyright © 2023 Ayla Cox

All rights reserved.
No part of this book may be reproduced or used in any form without the expressed and written permission of the copyright owner, except for the use of brief quotations for the purpose of book reviews and general shit-talking.

This is a work of fiction. Any similarity between characters and situations to people, living or dead, is unintentional and purely coincidental. If such similarities do exist within these pages, YOU GO, GLEN COCO, get your swerve on, bitch!

To reach Ayla, feel free to email her at:
AlyaCoxWrites@gmail.com.

ISBN:

DEDICATION

To G.
Everything became clear when you left.

TEMPTED

CONTENTS

ABOUT THIS BOOK..
PART 1 1
PART 2 27
ABOUT THE AUTHOR 67

ABOUT THIS BOOK

This book contains adult themes and activities, including some elements of BDSM that include sub/Dom power dynamics, spanking, restraints, and orgasm denial.

PART 1

As I looked around the party, I couldn't help but feel out of place. Clients and colleagues were all dressed in expensive clothes, dripping in fancy jewelry, and talking about their portfolios.
Someone had decided that Vivaldi was too stuffy, and Beyoncé was too progressive, but the string quartet version of Hypnotize by Biggie Smalls was perfect.

For the fourth time, a laugh bubbled up in my throat and I had to stuff that bitch down.

Biggie took what the world gave him and made something out of it. He used his pain to create music. I would've bet my bonus that no one in the room understood that. There was a gorgeous nuance of struggle and passion. They turned that into some one-percenter distortion and there I was, forced to pretend it was nice when a client asked about it.

I cleared my throat and focused on my feet. Not because it made me feel more grounded and at one with the earth, but because they hurt like a bitch and if I focused on the pain, I could focus on how great it would feel to kick them off in a little less than an hour.

Thankfully, I'd already worked the room and connected with all my clients. I even introduced a few that I knew would benefit from the expertise of other founders.

The sprawling ballroom was covered in galaxy-inspired artwork. Women wearing hoop skirts covered in cosmic cocktails floated by as entertainers dressed as various planets in our solar system worked the crowd.

It didn't escape me how odd it was for me to be wearing a thousand-dollar dress with eight-hundred-dollar shoes, holding a glass of champagne so expensive that it could've covered a month's worth of groceries for me five years ago.

This was the job I'd fought for, that I'd bled for and now in this room with billions of dollars, I wasn't excited. The extravagance and opulence, they just felt – odd.

Clients, on the other hand, were living their best lives. I watched them dive headfirst into everything the buffet had to offer.

"Cotton candy! I can definitely fit that in my bag, come on," a blond woman to my right squealed, grabbing someone's hand and making a run for the cotton candy vendor. She opened her bright purple Hermes handbag, which was already full of lamb skewers and roast chicken.

As I watched these people falling over themselves, I wondered if this was a life that I truly wanted for myself or if I was being blinded by the paychecks.

Taking a large sip, followed by another, I emptied the champagne flute and headed for the bar. Clearly, I was too sober and morose for this shit.

"Already heading back to the bar, Denny?"

I turned to see my plus-one traipsing up to me. Late. As. Fuck.

Morose was gone. It was quickly swallowed up by anger as I looked over Curtis, the man I'd been dating for nine years.

He'd thankfully chosen the suit I'd laid out for him and not whatever hoodie and jeans he could find lying around the closet. Normally I wouldn't give a shit what the man wore, but this was work, and Work Denny couldn't be caught looking unpolished, let alone arms linked with some low-rent B-Rabbit straight from the 8-Mile set.

"They say when the champagne is a hundred dollars a glass, demolish it," I said, pasting on a pleasant smile.

Curtis laughed and leaned in close.

"Is that what they say?" he asked.

"It could be. I haven't heard anyone say it tonight, but I'm sure it will catch on in this crowd." I chuckled, albeit hollowly, because who the fuck shows up two hours late to their girlfriend's work party.

I coolly led the way towards the bar, feeling the warmth of his guiding hand through my dress. I wasn't arguing in front of these white folks, especially the ones that signed my paychecks.

"Champagne, please. And he'll take a sparkling water."

The bartender turned to find glasses, and I dropped my used flute on the bar. Curtis raised his eyebrow, and I raised mine in silent conversation.

His eyebrow was asking about the water, mine was a reminder that he volunteered to drive us home, and he was far too late to have one drink if I was going to be out of these shoes in an hour.

"Denise!" I turned to see the one person I had hoped to avoid heading straight for me.

A fresh glass of champagne hit my hand as the Wicked Witch of the East air kissed my cheeks. Thank God the woman didn't come in for a hug, she smelled like oranges and musty leather.

"Gloria. Hi, I hope you're having a great evening."

She grabbed my arm.

"Isn't it so radiant? The galaxy theme really seems to be a hit with the clients. I'm so proud of what we were able to pull together."

I nodded. "It truly is special. My clients have been gushing about it all night."

She was a bitch, but she was also damn good at her job.

"I don't think we've met, I'm Gloria!" She reached her hand towards Curtis, who was holding at least two fingers of scotch, the fucking asshole.

"Oh, sorry! This is Curtis."

"The fiancé," he said crisply.

He said fucking *what*? I jolted and tried to cover it with a wide smile.

"Oh my god, I had no idea!" Gloria's eyes darted to my ring finger, which clearly didn't have an engagement ring on it.

"Ahh, it's a gorgeous solitaire cut. It's being resized right now, but I love it." Lying had become second nature in this place, but this was something else altogether.

"You have to show me when it comes back! I'm so happy for you. It was nice to meet you, *fiancé*. I've got to run. Have a lovely night, you two!"

She rushed off, and I was left standing beside Curtis, feeling winded as rage flooded my body. Thankfully, it did manage to distract me from the pain in my feet and I was able to storm – as much as one can storm in three-inch heels – toward the ladies' room without even acknowledging Curtis.

I threw back the full flute of champagne on the way, leaving the empty by the bathroom door.

Grabbing the corner stall, I took a deep and shaky breath. My therapist had explained that breathing into different areas of your body helped calm anxiety. But she never mentioned full-body rage. I didn't think that was going to be much help. But, murder? That would do the trick.

Closing my eyes, I thought about all the ways I could kill and get away with it. Water poisoning. I think that's a thing. Salt pills? No, that high blood pressure would take years, and I needed something immediate that drenched me in blood.

That made me feel better in a dark, very Cary Elwes in Saw kind of way. Squishy, slick blood. Warm and gooey. Nope, too far. I heaved a little at the thought and laughed. Yeah, that helped.

I took one final breath and opened the stall, ready to head back out.

A knock came at the bathroom door and a hand popped into view with a glass of champagne. Only one fool would be willing to embarrass himself by coming into the women's bathroom to check on me: Hugh.

Ensuring the other stalls were empty, I opened the door.

"The coast is clear, you can come in," I said, walking to the sink.

"You okay? It looked like you needed this."

I turned on the water and scrubbed my hands a bit harder than necessary while I sized up the impeccable one-button charcoal gray suit he was wearing in the mirror. It was all angles. He'd paired it with a crisp white button-up sans tie. Always on the daring side, three of the buttons were undone, and a golden jade bar winked against his honey umber skin. A highball glass of whiskey was gripped in his hand, and the word *snack* came to mind.

"Armani?" I asked, ignoring his question.

"Picked it up this morning, I didn't think it was going to be ready in time. Figured it would impress Lucian."

The CEO. He didn't need to impress Lucian. Hugh walked into the room and owned that bitch. He turned heads and charmed clients. And with this suit, he'd definitely received some stares. Perfectly tailored, it hung on Hugh like a second skin.

Hugh had started to grow out his heart-shaped beard, but he kept it shaped and tight. Seeing the fuller beard on him was something. It contrasted a bit with his bald head, but half the people he talked to didn't even notice because his charisma is what really caught your attention.

I dried my hands and grabbed the flute from him, feeling a zap of electricity as our fingers brushed. I shrugged it off and told my hormones to chill, a one-sided conversation we'd had many times before.

"It's definitely impressive," I said, smiling.

He smiled back. "This was all me, girl. And you – you look phenomenal."

The gown I'd gone with had a taupe collared silk top that connected to a flared-out blue, bronze, and silver metallic feathered skirt with a slit that came all the way up between my thighs. Sexy, but enough material to be a little modest. I'd tied the long sash around my waist to the side and finished off the chrome look with equally stunning smoky bronze and blue eyeshadow and a dark brown lip stain.

I took a lot of joy in dressing up for these events. Plus size clothing had changed so much in the last two decades and I felt like these events finally gave me the opportunity to lean in and try something new and different that didn't include dressing like a 75-year-old grandmother counting down her days.

I cleared my throat and sipped from my glass.

"It wasn't Gloria. Well, it wasn't *just* Gloria."

"Curtis?" Hugh asked, walking over to the bathroom door and flipping the lock.

Hugh had Char, I had Curtis. Neither of our partners really understood our work or what it was like to be a person of color in this world. How enraging just existing was in our office or at events like this. But Hugh and I had each other. We'd take a few minutes out of every day to sit and vent – about work, about life – his steady presence beside me was grounding.

I put the drink down and leaned against the sink to look at the ornate ceiling.

"He shows up so fucking late, he shouldn't have even bothered to come. And then he introduced himself as my fiancé to that woman."

Hugh made an incredulous noise and I continued.

"Imagine! The man hasn't had a job for a year, shows up late to the only event he had planned for the day, and now he wants to get married all of a sudden."

My voice went from conversational to a whispery screech in three seconds flat, and all that momentary relaxation I'd gained was gone.

"Okay. Okay." Hugh walked over. Putting down his drink, he grabbed my shoulders. "Hit me."

I startled. He gripped my waist, yanking me towards the middle of the room.

"Hit me. Kick me. Do whatever but get it out while we're in here. You are the worst compartmentalizer I've ever met. Don't even bother trying to calm down. Just, hit me."

Affronted, I gave him a look that read, *sir, you've lost your whole mind*.

"It'll make you feel better. I mean, obviously not the face." He crossed his forearms in front of him and peeked around them at me.

"Come on, do it. Don't be a candyass," he said, grabbing my limp arm.

A barking laugh came out of my mouth before I could stop it. I bent forward and cackled, feeling the pull from my diaphragm and the pressure in my lungs. I couldn't breathe. I looked up and saw Hugh's offended gaze before I doubled over and hit the ground, cackling.

Tears crept from my eyes as I grabbed my cramping stomach and tried to stop the laughter bubbling up. After a few seconds, I looked over to see Hugh crouched beside me waiting patiently for me to finish. His smile was gone and replaced by something else that I couldn't make sense of. I bit at my cheek and tried to take deep breaths to stop the giggles.

"'Don't be a candyass?'" I asked, wiping daintily at my eyes and looking down at the dress pooled around me.

"It worked, you're not a rage monster anymore," he said, holding out a hand to help me up.

I sighed and reached for him, teetering a bit on my heels as I gained my footing.

My fingers tightened around his biceps so I wouldn't fall on my face. They were firm, much firmer than I expected, so much so that I may have given them an extra squeeze after I gained my balance.

I dragged in a surprised breath and then laughed, trying to cover the fact that arms were apparently a turn-on for me now and his were – yummy.

"Oh, I'm a little –" I looked up to see Hugh staring down at me. Staring wasn't the right word – he was devouring me with his eyes. My words caught in my throat, and I leaned back against the sink.

"Denise, can I ask you something?" His voice was husky. He leaned closer, resting his hands on either side of the sink, caging me in. I could smell the whiskey on his lips mixed with his sandalwood and sage cologne. His scent was a welcoming fog, surrounding me, cushioning me, and pulling me closer to him.

"Sure." The words came out a whisper as I took in eyes the color of driftwood.

His finger flirted with the skin of my cheek and my breath caught.

Where the hell did this come from? I tried to swallow against the newly formed lump in my throat.

"Tell me you've never thought about me." He moved flush against my curves.

I'd be lying if I said I never thought of him that way. Of course, I had.

Hugh was temptation.

He was everything that made a man irresistible. Successful, impeccable, and polished, right down to his perfectly lined fade and jade cufflinks.

But he had Char and I had Curtis.

He leaned close, his scent enveloping me. I cleared my throat but didn't look away.

"That's not a question," I replied.

He leaned forward and my breath caught. But instead of kissing me, he brought his nose against mine, brushing gently against it. His hand moved to my neck, tracing along the edge of my collar. I let out a gasp as what felt like electricity began to follow his touch.

Hugh chuckled and I felt my face flush. His breath teased my earlobe before he ran his nose softly underneath my jaw. Heat began to course through me and pool in between my thighs. I fought the sudden urge to buck against his warm body.

I closed my eyes tight and tried to take a steadying breath to calm the mist of desire that was clouding me. His fingers traced my jaw and came to rest beside it.

"Do you want me to fuck you?"

The words were whispered against my lips. There, but not quite there. My heart thudded in my chest, beating hard against my ribs. I didn't know what to say, I couldn't think, all I could do was feel. My body was alight.

I didn't need to open my eyes to know that he still held that same heated look. The one that seemed to see me, see right into me.

"That was a question," he said. Unconsciously, I licked my bottom lip. A growl hummed in his chest, and I could feel the vibration in mine.

"You're drunk," I said, trying to keep myself in check, trying to temper my hormones, trying to tell my pussy to dry, and my feet to hold my weight and leave the bathroom. But instead, I let the scent of sage and sandalwood inebriate my senses while lust and champagne blurred my mind.

Lips traced my cheek and made a path towards my neck.

"You've had five glasses of champagne. Are you drunk?"

My tongue felt heavy in my mouth. He'd been counting? He'd been watching? I didn't respond.

Hugh tutted.

"Are you?" he asked again, more firmly.

"No," I replied.

Every breath I took made my breasts brush against him.

"Neither am I," he said, grabbing my waist and effortlessly placing me on the edge of the sink before taking a step back.

"I'm waiting for you to answer my question."

Hugh may have put distance between us, but the heat was still there, burning my skin and gripping me tight. Hugh's hands went into his pockets, and I couldn't help but stare at the bulge tenting at the front of his slacks.

I opened my mouth to speak, but nothing came out. I tried again, but I couldn't think, not with the idea of being spread open and demolished by this man in my head. I crossed my legs, trying to ease the pressure on my core. It didn't work, but it did bring Hugh's attention to my thighs, now in full view beneath the dress.

I could almost feel his eyes as his gaze slowly caressed every inch of my exposed skin, falling on the apex where the dress stopped mere inches from my heat.

"Yes." The ragged and needy sound came from my mouth. Before I could slow my tongue, I continued, "I want you to fuck me."

Hugh unbuttoned and shrugged off his suit jacket, his eyes never leaving mine. I leaned back, watching as he moved.

"Not here," he said, throwing it over a stall door. He removed his cufflinks and started to fold up the sleeves of his shirt, ending at his elbows and leaving behind toned forearms.

His right arm was covered in an intricate, weaving design that crawled past his shirt. It started a little above his wrist, and knowing Hugh, it was no doubt designed specifically to hide beneath his shirt. If you wanted to be taken seriously in Corporate America, you had to assimilate and be creative with self-expression.

Hugh began closing the distance between us. I couldn't help but feel like I was being hunted – stalked. My heart started to pound, and I didn't blink, I didn't move.

The noise from the party faded, and it was just us, just that moment in time. When he got close, he paused. A moment of quiet passed between us, him standing just out of reach, his hands back in his pockets.

I paused, unsure if he was having second thoughts or if he was waiting for something from me.

"Hugh?" I said, starting to feel self-conscious.

"I'm taking it in," he said, scanning me slowly, head to toe.

"Really?" I laughed.

"The power you have strolling around the room in this dress, that – energy."

I felt a blush creep up my neck, and I grabbed at his belt loops, dragging him forward. He took the hint, his warm hands splayed across my thighs, and I moaned as he uncrossed and nestled between them.

One hand found its way to my breast through my dress, while the other gripped my throat and pulled me close.

"Just a taste," he whispered, before leaning forward and claiming my mouth.

Our lips moved in a slow, sensual rhythm. But when my hands gripped his hips, it was like a switch flipped.

The kiss changed from tender to hungry, from smoldering to a fire. His hand tilted my head as his tongue pushed forward, exploring, plundering in a way that left me aching and wanting more. His rhythm was bruising. I dug my hands into his sides to stay upright.

I could taste the whiskey as he sucked my tongue into his mouth. The hand on my breast moved to pop open the button at the top of my collar, exposing my chest. His hand explored my skin and I hissed against his mouth, pulling him closer.

Through the cascade of sensations, my thoughts started to whirl. While a part of me needed and wanted this, the other part knew it was a bad idea. Knew that there was a line I was crossing that couldn't be uncrossed, and it could have disastrous effects. But I wanted to give in to this. I had a right to feel, and this made me feel good. Hugh made me feel good.

He popped another button open, his hand moving under my shirt, sliding to my bra-covered breast. He palmed its weight, and I felt him exhale into my mouth, as he nipped and pulled at my lips with his teeth. His forefinger and thumb closed on my breast, pulling. I sighed as his mouth moved to my jaw.

"Is this okay?" Hugh whispered against my skin. I nodded and Hugh tutted. "Use your words," he said.

There was something delicious about this. My senses were heightened, it was so intense and intimate, and I was craving everything he could give me.

"Yes, more," I said, forcing the words out. Fingers closed in tighter, pulling harder. I cried out as ecstasy mingled with the pain.

I gasped, feeling slick wetness begin to pool in my panties. I needed more. I pressed into his fingers, offering myself to him, ravenous. His teeth nipped at my neck as his fingers gripped tight and pulled again, harder and longer.

My hands went to his shoulders as waves of pleasure and pain rocked me. I bit my cheek, trying hard to muffle the sounds being drawn from me.

Hugh's tongue continued to play along the skin of my neck, alternating between licking and biting. Everything I felt went right to my pussy. Trying to ease the throbbing, I squeezed my thighs together again, hoping for relief. With Hugh standing between them, I couldn't get the pressure where I wanted it.

Hugh's hand moved from my neck and cupped me through my panties, groaning. He leaned back, his eyes burrowed into mine before he kissed me again.

My heart was thumping in my skin. I was high on him. On this. The way his touch alternated between rough and sensual had me gasping for air.

I grasped at him, finding the edge of his pants, and feeling for the zipper. I wanted to feel him beneath me.

Hugh gripped my hands, stopping them.

"Not here," he repeated. "When I fuck you, I want you alone."

"Then what?" I asked, feeling slighted.

His lips landed on mine again, lightly sucking and nipping, while his hand simultaneously dipped into my panties and tore them from underneath my dress. I gasped, feeling the cool air against my aching, wet lips.

"One," he whispers against my skin.

His hand slowly caressed the folds of my pussy, and I leaned into him, only for him to lift his hand away.

"You get one, but we have to be careful."

I groaned in dismay, and he chuckled, moving his lips and tongue down my exposed chest, tracing the edge of my bra.

"Do you want me to stop?"

I shook my head. He paused, raising his eyebrows. "No," I said.

"Open your mouth," he said. He took my panties and held them up.

My stomach clenched. "Yes," I said before he could ask, opening my mouth for him.

He traced over my lips with the lace before his thumb pulled at my bottom lip and teased the tip of my tongue. Pushing the fabric inside, he closed my lips around them. He looked at me, his smile wolfish.

"Quiet, you don't want anyone to hear."

He placed a kiss against my lips as his hand continued its caress, this time his fingers parted my pussy lips and began exploring.

I sucked in a hard breath, biting against the bundled cloth and panting. My body began to shudder at the mixed feeling of his lips sucking, licking, and nipping my neck and the lightest touch of his hand against me.

I pushed against him, needing more. His other hand found the perfect spot on my abdomen, placing firm pressure that filled me with pleasure.

I felt fluid. Every move in our dance was stoking the flames higher and teasing me more and more. I arched against him again, moaning.

He shushed against my skin, finally moving his questing fingers up to my clit.

His lips drifted to my earlobe and bit down before he started whispering, voice gravelly, deeper than I'd ever heard it.

"You like that, don't you?" he asked, his fingers rolling over my clit, once, then twice before diving low and exploring the wetness dripping down my thighs.

"Yes," I agreed.

"Do you want my fingers to fuck that tight pussy of yours?"

I cried out as I felt two of his fingers plunge into me. I felt my walls clench down, milking him. He pushed into me once before pausing.

"What's the rule?"

He leaned back, looking into my eyes. I rocked into him, feeling rushing waves of bliss.

"Ah, ah." He pulled out and I gasped. "What's the rule? Say it."

"Quiet," I replied, the word muffled but intelligible.

I couldn't think of anything but his hands on me and in me.

"That's right. We can't play if you don't follow the rules. Can you follow the rules?"

"Yes," I nod, feeling more turned on than I'd felt in years.

"And what's the magic word?" he asked against my lips.

"Please," I replied, and was immediately rewarded when his fingers plunged back inside me. I bit my cheek and held firm.

"And what do you say?"

"Thank you." I managed, grunting as his fingers thrust in and out, building a rhythm. I was trying so hard to stay quiet as he brought me higher and higher. I grabbed onto his hips, trying to ground myself as my eyes closed. I was lost in it, moving my hips with every thrust of his fingers.

My breath caught in my throat at the relentless pace of his thick fingers fucking in and out of me. His thumb circled my clit as he reached up and angled deeper.

I was delirious with the need to cum. I couldn't think, I couldn't breathe. The panties were pulled from my mouth and Hugh's mouth caught mine, kissing me with the same relentless force that he was building with his fingers.

"That's it, beautiful," he said, biting at my lip before returning to his bruising kisses, swallowing my cries as my body tightened and exploded. What felt like a hot, bright light exploded, and I shuddered, feeling euphoric. I gasped as Hugh covered my face with kisses.

His fingers didn't stop pumping into me as I shook and continued to fuck his fingers. It was so good that I couldn't stop, I didn't want to stop. I grabbed his face, claiming his mouth as his fingers stoked me higher, thrusting deep.

"Please, please, please," I begged against his lips. "Keep going."

I felt another orgasm building. I was mindless. My body was doing things, I was saying things, and Hugh was there with me stroke after stroke. He changed it up, rotating and moving in an unpredictable pattern that had me sighing in search of my release.

"I'm not stopping, gorgeous."

His words egged me on as I began rolling my hips against him. My hands went to his shoulders, pulling him closer, knowing what I really wanted was him pumping in and out of me with more than his fingers. The second orgasm was just there, right on the edge, I could almost taste it. I moved harder and faster against him. I wanted it. I needed it. I deserved it.

"That's it, fuck my fingers. You're drenching them." His fingers were pounding into me, and I swore I was close, but I couldn't get there. I couldn't cum. I groaned in frustration.

Hugh kissed me, his fingers circling and squeezing my clit tightly. Blinding heat stilled me as I orgasmed, my pussy gushing against my thighs, coating them in my juices.

I came so hard that I felt the edges of my sight blackening as I fell back, my fingers finding purchase in my dress, grabbing at the fabric, and riding each wave. I don't know who I was, but it wasn't Denny. I was outside of myself, pulled out from the sheer force of the climax.

My body, high on lust and endorphins, was floating. After what felt like forever, I realized I was lying motionless on the sink, the only thing I could feel was my chest moving, dragging in the air my burning lungs demanded.

It was incredible. Hugh was – incredible. Everything about him was new, different, and fucking addictive. It took two tries to sit up. Hugh was crouching down, a broken champagne and highball glass were scattered across the ground. It smelled like liquor.

"We made a little bit of a mess. I got it," he said, glancing at me but keeping his focus on the handful of broken glass he was holding.

I couldn't even pretend like I would be helpful right now. I was liquid and liquid I was planning to stay.

After a minute or so, the clinking stopped, and I looked up to see Hugh standing over me, just watching.

"Hmm," I managed to get out as I leaned onto my forearms to get a better look at him.

His shirt was back in place, and he was fastening his cufflinks back to his wrists.

"We're not finished," he said.

I laughed because I definitely felt finished.

"Here's what's going to happen. You're going to get rid of Curtis, tell him you need to head back to work, and that you'll see him at home. Then, you're going to meet me in my office, and I'm going to fuck you so hard, you're going to tell your girls you met God, Allah, and Yahweh spread across a desk."

The way his tone shifted told me that he was serious.

He wasn't done, and he really planned to make me keep coming. I didn't see how it was possible, but I twinged at the thought.

"Or. You could go home and pretend that boring vanilla shit is good enough. We can pretend like this never happened and I can go back to being your work husband and partner-in-crime."

I leaned forward and slid off the sink, holding on until I was sure I had my balance back. I walked slowly towards Hugh, my fingers buttoning my dress. When I reached him, my fingers traced the jade hanging from his neck.

"You think because you made me cum a few times, you can tell me what to do?"

It was his turn to laugh, he stepped closer, his thumb caressing my bottom lip.

"Open your mouth," he said.

I raised my eyebrows, and he tilted his head in question.

"I said, open your mouth." The words were a demand, a decree. His eyes were serious and before I could stop myself, I opened my mouth.

He placed his fingers inside, the tangy taste hit my taste buds as he mimicked what he'd just done to my pussy.

"Good girl," he said, a savage smile lifting his lips.

I was euphoric, his words created a pleasant buzz in my head and turned me the fuck on. I wanted him to say it again.

His gaze never left mine as his fingers moved in and out of my mouth, gliding across my tongue. He pushed them forward, reaching a bit too far, making me gag.

Leaning forward, he rubbed his nose against mine.

"I think you want someone to see you and to fuck your mouth raw."

Before I could react, he claimed my mouth, his tongue sucking, his teeth biting. I shivered, keeping up with each stroke of his tongue, before he abruptly stepped back and looked down at me.

"I can tell you what to do because you love this. You're curious. And you want more. See you in twenty." He spun on his heel, grabbed his suit jacket, and strolled out of the bathroom.

I could hear him through the door, "Oh, I'm sorry, ma'am. Can you believe I walked into the wrong restroom? I scared that poor woman to death and dropped my drink in my rush to leave. May want to watch your step as you come inside. I think I got all the glass, but I'm on my way to grab an attendant to clean up."

I barely had time to pick up my jaw off the floor as someone breezed in and looked from the ground to me.

"Men," she said with a laugh, heading for a stall.

"Yeah, men," I breathed, holding tight to my somersaulting stomach and looking at my flushed face in the mirror.

Men in-fucking-deed.

I spent the next five minutes sitting in the very comfy chair conveniently placed outside of the bathroom. When I closed my eyes, I could still smell him, still feel his strong grip on my thighs, holding me open against the cold marble of the sink. My lips were still puffy and sensitive, I licked them again, enjoying the pleasure it gave me.

Hugh had given me a choice. Options that felt straightforward and simple, but he knew it wasn't simple. Not with the way that we responded to one another. He woke up something inside of me that I didn't know existed.

Dared me to think about myself, my pleasure, taking and giving control. Because control is what it was about. I was in charge all the time because I knew that the safety I craved most wouldn't be found relying on anyone else.

Today, I felt safe, I gave in to something and it cracked open a door. I could shut it, or I could kick it open. I had to decide, and I had to decide now.

Taking a steeling breath, I stood, tearing forward, determined.

I smiled and waved as I walked, scanning the crowded room for Curtis. It took me a few minutes, but I finally spotted him. He was talking with a few of my colleagues, smiling and being the social butterfly, he was born to be. An hour ago, I would've charged over, hoping to prevent him from saying something that could embarrass me, but I sat back and watched him chat.

This wasn't the Curtis that I saw every day. The one in sweats, gaming headset on, screaming into a microphone thirteen hours a day while the mess piled up around him. This Curtis was easy to smile and charming. When he spotted me, the smile faded, and he excused himself, walking over to meet me.

"You've been gone for almost forty-five minutes." He said, his tone admonishing.

"A client has an emergency. We chatted about what they need, but I have to head back to the office." The lie came easier than I expected it to.

"This was supposed to be our night. I've been looking forward to it." Curtis slammed back the rest of his drink and I placed my hand on his arm. It was the same story as always, why was I ruining his fun?

No mention of the fact that he was late or that this party was for my career. It was my opportunity to connect with clients and further grow partnerships. Clients that I had to keep to pay for the electricity and Wi-Fi he gamed on all day while he "looked" for the perfect job.

My smile was wooden as I grabbed his empty glass from his hands and placed it down on a table. It wasn't lost on me that when my hand grazed his there were no fireworks, no marching band was playing in my body, no flutter in my soul.

The party was still in full swing and would be until the early morning, but he didn't need to know that. All he needed to see was the inside of a cab.

"I'm so sorry. Walk me out? Did you drive?" I pulled him gently, and he walked with me, side by side, through the throng of people and out into the cold night air.

"I took a ride-share," he said, sounding affronted. Of course, he didn't drive like we'd agreed.

"Let's get you a cab."

The city was breezy, whipping past me and making me shiver. I hugged my abdomen and thanked the heavens that a line of taxis was waiting across the street from the hotel.

I waved at the one closest to us. The driver waved back and hopped in, turning on the engine and doing a U-turn to pull up in front of us.

"I shouldn't have snapped at you. I know your work is important." Curtis sounded sincerely apologetic. But, as usual, it was for all the wrong things. I rubbed his arm as he opened the taxi door.

"We can talk in the morning," I said.

"Yeah," he mumbled, sliding into the back of the cab. His dejection was laid on too thick. He'd expect an apology from me when I got home – something to make up for work coming between us.

I bit my lip and took a breath, keeping all of the words and all of the commentary I had to myself. I closed the cab door and started to trek up the street.

There was someplace I needed to be.

PART 2

It took me five minutes to walk from the hotel back to the office. Foxx Ventures took the top two floors of one of the tallest and newest buildings in San Francisco. I pushed against heavy doors and sighed as the heat surrounded me.

My hands went to my arms in an attempt to rub some life back into them as I looked around the almost empty lobby. It was opulent and over the top, exactly like Julian liked it. I waved at the guard sitting behind his desk, and a delighted smile crossed his face.

"Well, if it isn't my favorite! I thought you all had that shindig tonight." Bill was one of those hip older folks, he was always talking about the funny videos he found online or the newest addition he'd made to a computer he was building at home.

"There is. I have a few things I need to get to before the weekend, so I ducked out a little early."

Bill shook his head, "They work you too hard. Hugh went up maybe twenty minutes ago."

I feigned surprise. "Really?"

Bill nodded as I placed my palm against the barrier, and it scanned my handprint.

"I'll give his office a ring in case anyone heads up after you." Bill laughed as I clutched at invisible pearls.

This was our game. Only it didn't really feel like a game at that moment.

"We're colleagues, Bill," I said, with the least amount of conviction I had ever been able to muster. After all, the man's fingers had just been inside me.

"I'm just saying, you two may as well make it official." He winked and turned back to his monitors as I released a breath, I didn't realize I was holding.

Bill always gave Hugh and me a hard time when he saw us together. I always saw it as a joke, but it meant something more today, knowing what I was going to do. The elevator furthest from me opened and I stepped inside.

One of the perks of being in a fancy building is the elevator screen greeted me by name and displayed 60, rocketing up. As the floors ticked by, I suddenly felt nervous. All that talk about wanting to feel good and doing something for me started to sound hollow.

My desire had cooled on the way here, probably partly due to the brisk wind and that conversation I'd had with Curtis. What if this was a mistake? What if I just needed to go home, tell Curtis that he needed to do better, or leave?

I rubbed my sweaty palms on my dress and the elevator slowed to a stop and opened. I looked out at the dark hall and stared.

This was the moment.

I had to choose whether I was committing to this.

The idea of it, the feel of it was – phenomenal.

The way Hugh tempted me, showed me something I didn't realize I wanted and needed.

But who was I at that moment? It wasn't me to cheat, let alone cheat with someone I had to see every single day. Someone important to me that I couldn't foresee myself losing.

The elevator doors started to close, and I stopped them. I looked at the doors and asked myself a simple question, the same one I'd been thinking earlier that night: what did I deserve?

I looked down at my dress, a dress I would have never thought I would be able to afford, and I stepped off the elevator.

I deserved whatever the fuck I wanted.

Right now, I wanted something new and different and wild, and I was going to get it.

The elevator snapped shut behind me, leaving me shrouded in shadow. My heels clicked against the marble floor as I pressed my palm over the wall and the door unlocked.

I yanked off my heels and traversed the carpeted open floor plan. The design of the office was all angles and muted blues and grays, but it lacked any real personality.

The cubicles were ashen ivory and were just high enough to encourage colleagues to remain focused on work instead of socializing. I'd spent two years working at one before I was finally able to secure my own office.

Turning the corner, I walked into my office, dropped my heels on the desk, and looked out at the city. Being this high, nestled in the clouds, made me feel like absolutely anything was possible.

The day that I was promoted and given this office, Hugh and I spent a week straight sitting at this window and taking it all in. Three of those nights, Karl the fog rolled in and shrouded the city, but that didn't stop us from demolishing six bottles of champagne, chatting and laughing about life.

My fingers found their way back to my lips, still sensitive from Hugh's bruising kisses. The longer I stood there, feeling like I was on top of the world, the bolder I felt. A plan started to form.

I left my heels and padded two doors down to Hugh's corner office. The light was coming through the door. It was dim, but I felt drawn to it like a moth. *There's a joke about Icarus here*, I thought, as I walked in.

His office, unlike the rest of the floor, felt masculine. Photos of him and a few founders lined his bookshelf, along with plaques that commemorated the date of their exit. This was the dream – facilitating an exit for a phenomenal startup with the right supportive investors – and he'd already done it so many times.

Hugh was standing at his panoramic view, looking out at the Bay.

"Ruminating on your plans to take out 007?" I asked, moving to stand beside him.

He let out a low chuckle. "I was thinking about the first time I met you. You walked in, almost like you were apologizing. John called you Denisha and you let the beast out."

Now it was my turn to laugh. The man had thought it was a funny joke.

"That man learned that day. And I had the honor of making Shana from HR's acquaintance after I eviscerated him."

"He ordered fries, and you gave him a combo," Hugh said.

"And supersized it."

We laughed and I was relieved. Things were different now, but they were still the same. Speaking of the same, we needed to talk before everything started.

"I have terms," I said.

"Of course, that's expected," Hugh replied and turned to look at me.

"This is all a little–"

"Kinky."

"Kinky," I agreed. "I mean, I love the element of surprise, but we should talk about it."

"We can do that. What else?"

I put a little distance between us and started to pace. This was going to be a harder sell, especially with the way he kept staring at my mouth instead of making eye contact.

"I think we should put a clock on it. Tonight. Just tonight." I turned and watched a flash of hurt cross his face before his face went blank.

"You're having second thoughts –"

"No, no. I'm not." I walked over and stopped myself from reaching for him, wringing my hands in front of me instead.

"You're important to me and I value us. I don't want that to change. We take one night, put everything out on the table, and then Monday morning it's business as usual." I spoke quickly, trying to be specific and honest and hoping that he understood my reasoning.

Hugh was quiet as he turned his gaze back out the window.

The silence was hanging between us, and I fought hard not to fill it. Instead, I looked back out at the city glinting below us.

Even though the night was breezy and unusually cold, it was clear, and I could see past Belvedere Island.

"Two," Hugh said, his eyes continuing to scan the city skyline, deep in thought. "Two nights. Tonight, and another night of our choosing."

Rules were working for me. Negotiating helped me shake out the nerves and see this as it was: a business deal with a side of orgasms. Having this conversation, putting parameters around this, it was – hot?

I tried not to think too hard about that and focused on the idea of two days of this. The searing fire between us that hadn't seemed to die down. Just looking at Hugh, watching his lips draw together, his hand smoothing his jacket.

Two could work.

Hell, we hadn't even fucked yet, and the man had already made me come quicker than anyone ever had.

"Two it is," I replied.

Hugh strode over to his desk and took a seat, gesturing to the other across from him. I sat down and he leaned across the desk.

"You can always change your mind." Hugh's voice was firm. I nodded.

This was Negotiation Hugh. I straightened my back. "Okay."

"We need two safe words: one to slow down, one to stop."

"What's wrong with slow down and stop?" I asked, confused.

"Ambiguity. Slower could mean this is too much. Or slower could mean, this is delicious, go slower." Hugh's fingers found mine. His fingertips began to slowly stroke each of my fingers.

"I see. Let me think?"

Hugh smiled, his tongue peeking out to wet his lips. "Take your time," he said, continuing his slow caresses that were transmitting electricity straight through me.

"Grapefruit, for slow," I said, gasping as his fingers stroked my wrist.

"Grapefruit for slow," Hugh repeated, keeping his focus on me.

"Habanero, for stop."

"Habanero for stop." Hugh echoed, his hand slowly moving up my arm.

I cleared my throat and looked towards the open office door.

"Should I close that?" I asked.

"Please. I can pour us a drink if you'd like."

I nod, practically leaping from the chair, my fingers covering the skin where his had been moments before.

"Use your words."

A shiver shot right to my center.

I contemplated obeying, but as my hands pushed the door shut, I realized I didn't have to.

"Or what?" I asked, turning around to look at him. My heart beat a little faster. Hugh paused at the liquor cabinet, one hand on his whiskey and the other on two glasses. He was quiet for a moment before he pulled out a single glass and closed the cabinet.

"Misbehaving already. Interesting."

He filled his glass and took a swig before pulling off his jacket.

"It's not misbehaving, it's inquiry. I'm curious about the rules." I said, knowing full well what the rules were. I was the prey. He was the hunter.

Hugh smiled, the same feral smile he'd had in the restroom. "Good girls get rewards. Bad girls get punished." He moved slowly towards me. "You get one freebie. I'm feeling generous after your pussy milked my fingers. On your knees."

Looking down at my dress, I dropped to my knees, being careful not to crush the fabric. Hugh stood there watching for a moment, a pleased look on his face. He took one last sip before placing his glass on the desk and closing the gap between us. His fingers found and lifted my chin.

I was gazing up at him towering over me, and goosebumps broke out across my skin. I wanted more of this. Of him.

His thumb traced my lip before palming my cheek and gently pushing my hair to the side. His hand went to undo and remove his belt and pull down his zipper. I licked my lips.

"One tap for yes, two taps for no. Repeat it." He said as his thumb caressed my cheek.

"One for yes, two for no," I say, trying to keep eye contact and failing as his hand moved into his pants to free himself.

Women always talk about magnificent dick like they're Captain Ahab, searching for an elusive white whale. Maybe it was sheer need, maybe it was the thick, gleaming pole in front of me, but I understood. Magnificent didn't feel like a proper description, it was perfection.

That same little voice told me to make him squirm, to take my time before I gave him what he wanted. I took him in my hands, my fingers grazing his soft, velvety skin. He was hot and hard. When my fingers tightened around him, it jumped in my hands. His length was as long as my palm. I couldn't wait to taste him at the back of my throat.

I licked my lips and looked up at Hugh, his hungry eyes were looking down at me, watching. Moving my hand to my mouth, I licked my palm before returning it to his shaft, moving slowly down his skin, feeling the heat beneath my fingers.

I pulled down again, slowly moving towards the head of his dick, taking satisfaction in the hiss I heard from above. I thumbed his head, wiping the sticky pre-cum across his opening.

My fingers moved back up, tracing the veins bulging beneath his skin. When I reached the base, I cupped the weight of his balls, feeling them move beneath his skin. He still hadn't budged, but I could feel his gaze burning through me.

Leaning forward, I opened my mouth and licked a vein, tracing it down and making a circle at the base of his dick, my tongue teasing his balls. Hugh gave a throaty chuckle, and I looked up.

"You're teasing me," he said, his voice low and heavy.

"Is it working?"

He laughed, his hand moving into my hair as he leaned down, so we were face to face.

I captured his mouth, my tongue tangling with his, my hand finding a smooth rhythm moving up and down his length. He moaned into my mouth, his lips crashing into mine as his grip on my hair tightened. Pulling away, his nose grazed mine.

"I think you should take what you want."

I did just that. Opening my mouth, I took as much of him as I could.

Hugh swore above me as I sucked hard, pulling all the way back before filling my mouth again. He tasted salty and tangy. I wanted more. His hands found my hair again, holding tight as my mouth worked up and down. I pulled back, focusing on the head of his dick, alternating between sucking the skin and running my tongue around it.

More pre-cum beaded at his head and I sucked and licked it away, taking him as deep as I could again, my tongue flattening against the underside of his length.

"Good. That's good. Give me your hand." He took hold of my other hand, placing it at his base.

"Hold it there," he said, his fingers tightening in my hair. "Now open your throat."

I took a deep breath and opened my mouth, relaxing my tongue. He pulled my head slowly back and forth, controlling the pace. I flicked my tongue on him as he dragged himself all the way out of my mouth and thrust back in.

"You okay?" he asked, groaning. I tapped once against his thigh, squeezing it.

"Your mouth feels amazing," he said, pulling tighter on my hair, his hips starting to slowly thrust back and forth.

My thighs were wet from all the heat between my legs. I went to move the hand on his thigh and his hand covered mine.

"Look at me."

I met his eyes, my mouth full of him.

"Keep it there. In case you want me to stop."

I grunted my dislike, tightening my thighs against my swollen flesh and enjoying the pressure. He looked down at me and raised his eyebrows. I patted his thigh once. I felt his dick jolt in my mouth.

"That's my good girl."

There it was again. I exhaled and tightened my thighs again.

His hips abandoned the slow pace and began a quick and swift rhythm, drawing him in and out of my mouth. I couldn't keep up the teasing I was doing with my tongue, so I hummed, pulling him in and taking as much of him as I could. Saliva started to drip down my chin as he pulled in and out of my mouth. I tasted more of his pre-cum on my tongue.

"Yes. Like that." Hugh hissed through his teeth. His hips thrusted him further into my mouth as his groans started to get louder.

"I'm gonna cum." He grunted each word as both hands grabbed at my head, using my mouth.

He tried to pull free, but my hand grabbed his ass, holding tight.

It was my turn. I took over the rhythm, slurping and sucking, pulling him in and out of my mouth, enjoying the symphony he was making above me mixed with the wet sounds he was making in my mouth.

I moved my tongue side to side, licking at the bottom of his shaft, while I bobbed my head backward and forward. Hugh cried out, spilling his cum down my throat.

Humming, I sucked hard as he groaned. He cursed as I did it again and again. After the fifth trip down, he hissed and pulled from my mouth with a pop.

Hugh sank to his knees in front of me and grabbed me by the throat.

His eyes looked glassy, and he was out of breath. I gave him a small smile and he smiled back.

"I think you just sucked out my soul," he said before kissing me, thrusting his tongue in slowly, tightening his grip on my throat.

I laughed against his lips as he nudged my thighs open. His fingers went right to my nub. My laugh turned into a cry.

"Mhm, I knew you'd be wet for me," he said, pulling my clit between two fingers and kissing me hard. He scissored his fingers, pulling and flicking as my orgasm began to build. I panted as he started to kiss my face.

My hips jerked against his hand, trying to gain more friction. He was turning me inside out. I just needed a little more.

"Please," I whispered.

Hugh tutted against my neck before pulling his hand away.

I gasped, opening my eyes to see him looking down at me, his fingers in his mouth.

"I want to taste you when you cum. Get on the desk." Hugh stood, offering me his hand.

He adjusted himself back into his suit pants as he started walking me backward toward the desk.

"Wait," he said, carefully grabbing at the sash tied at my waist. Pulling, he undid the knot, sliding the fabric open. He then worked each button free, his fingers caressing my chest as he went. He pushed one side of my dress off, and then the other, gently holding the fabric as he pulled it over my hips.

Once I was free, he lifted it and placed it over two chairs, his fingers lingering on the chiffon.

Standing at the edge of his large desk, my bare ass perched, I waited. I'd gone with my favorite long-line lace bra, a blue that matched the dress. A bra he'd barely looked at because he was treating the dress with such reverence.

When Hugh turned, he found me smirking.

"What?" he asked.

"You treated that dress very respectfully," I replied.

Hugh tilted his head and strolled back over to me, taking me in, inch by inch. I couldn't help but squirm under his unflinching stare.

"It looked remarkable on you, but I like you like this too." His hands touched my bare thighs and slowly traveled up towards my waist.

I cleared my throat and pulled him closer, but he resisted.

"There. That's your tell."

"My tell?" I asked, confused.

"Whenever you're uncomfortable, you clear your throat and misdirect. But you get this little pleased smile. A shadow of one, but it's there." Hugh angled my face up to his.

"I – no, I don't." I scoffed and tried to turn away, but he wouldn't let me.

"Let's try this again. You lit the room up tonight. Heads turned when you walked by. One of my clients asked me who you were."

I laughed but Hugh didn't.

"Denise. Say thank you," he said, using the same no-bullshit tone he'd used earlier.

"Thank you," I said, breathless.

"Good girl," he whispered.

Butterflies exploded in my stomach. Honest to God, fucking butterflies. His hand came up, his lips caressed my cheek.

"Alright, where were we?" he asked, grabbing me around the middle and pulling me up on the desk. Leaning over, he grabbed his whiskey, pushing everything else onto the ground with a sweep of his arm.

"I've always wanted to do that."

We laughed, me leaning up against him while he kicked off his shoes.

He poured a bit more whiskey into his glass before closing the bottle and putting it away.

"I bribed Bill. He'll call if anyone comes back from the party." Hugh said, taking a sip.

"Of course, you did," I said, my fingers going to his chest, feeling the warmth of his skin through his shirt.

"Want a taste?" Hugh asked, offering me his glass.

I reached for the glass as he tilted his hand, spilling across my thigh.

"Hugh!" I went to wipe it away when his hand stilled mine. I looked up and saw a gleam in his eyes. He'd done it on purpose.

"Oops," he said. "Let me get that."

Putting his glass down, he winked before dropping to his knees in front of me. His hands found the sides of my thighs as he placed an open kiss on one knee and then the other.

A shiver of anticipation ran through me.

Hugh's hands caressed my thighs, gliding slowly over my skin, gently feeling with the tips of his fingers. He started placing open-mouth kisses along my skin, moving slowly up my thigh, inching his way up toward the whiskey he'd spilled.

My skin was alight, each kiss, stoking me higher and higher, as his beard tickled my skin, and his soft lips worked their magic. I let out a sigh, my hands holding tight to the edge of the desk beneath me. Hugh was dedicated to his task, but his eyes never left mine.

The eye contact added to my intoxication. I was lost in him as his warm breath continued to tease my sensitive skin.

With a triumphant sound, he reached the drizzle of whiskey. His tongue darted out, gently licking the wet trail. A gasp escaped my lips as he flattened his tongue across my skin and sucked.

The room seemed to fade away as I felt desire building again in my belly.

Hugh's hands held tight on my thighs as he sucked and tongued my skin.

My breaths were coming faster, and I wanted more, needed more. I reached down, feeling the swollen lips of my pussy and finding my clit when Hugh stopped me.

"Ah, ah, this is mine." He said, stopping and leaning back.

"I can see the confusion, let me help." He walked around his desk, opening a drawer. I sat up as he pulled out two of his spare ties, one black and embossed with gold, the other paisley blue.

He couldn't mean? My stomach dipped. I tried to swallow but couldn't.

Hugh paused in front of me for a moment, his hand finding my cheek as he watched my face. "This is for you as much as me."

I trusted him, but this was giving him something that I normally kept a tight hold on.

The idea of letting him tie me down was thrilling and sexy, but my brain wasn't sure losing that control would work for me. But, with my safe words, I was only giving away control until I wanted to have it back.

"Yes." The word came out with more conviction than I felt.

Hugh grabbed my right hand, kissing the inside of my wrist as he tied one end of a tie to it. Grabbing my left hand, he did the same. He slipped his fingers between the silk and my skin.

"Are these too tight?" he asked, tugging a bit.

"No," I whispered, licking my lips.

Hugh groaned before his mouth collided with mine, his hands framing my face as his tongue dived deep, sucking and pulling against my tongue. I tugged at his beard, running my fingers along his skin.

He pushed me flat against the desk beneath us. His weight against me felt divine. I tilted my hips. He moaned into my mouth. I did it again, this time, I reached down to grab an ass cheek to pull him tighter to me.

Exhaling, he grabbed my hand and put it above my head, pulling the other up to join it. I leaned forward, biting his lips. Hugh cursed, pulling away and quickly pulling and looping at the ties before leaning back.

"Good, now I can take my time. And, you can't cause any more trouble," he said, his hands moving down my chest.

He slowly traced the fabric of my bra, smiling as I shuddered.

Hugh found and lifted his whiskey, dripping across my neck before leaning down and sipping it from my skin, biting before sucking and licking at the sting.

I was drowning in desire.

More liquid hit my skin as Hugh's weight shifted. His tongue traced down my stomach, taking time to swirl across my skin, teeth nipping as his lips sucked.

I tightened my thighs, need making my pussy heavy. Hugh laughed against my skin.

"Someone's eager," he mocked.

He moved back to his place on the floor, his hands running down my thighs. I glanced down, seeing Hugh staring up at me, his gaze mischievous.

He was enjoying this torture. So was I. Every nerve in my body was awake and turned the fuck on. As much as I loved this, I wanted him – no, I needed him to touch me and take me higher. My head fell back, and a long sigh escaped me as he licked my thigh, moving closer to where I craved him most.

A finger entered my pussy. I cried out in pleasure and relief. I bucked against it, but he held me to the desk. His tongue slowly moved down, replacing his finger and spearing into me, twirling around and around, lapping at my juices.

"Yes, please. More." I called out, exhaling, fingers twisting against the ties.

Hugh's hands came up and held me tight under his ravaging and talented tongue.

Each thrust showed that he was taking his time, savoring me as he teased my clit.

My cries started to echo around the office as I bucked against him, unable to keep still. His grip tightened as he continued assaulting my pussy.

The orgasm crested and stole my breath. I was overcome. He continued to suck my clit with the same slow, methodical pressure.

When he added another finger, going slower, I felt like I was floating.

"Hugh." He looked at me, his beard glistening.

"Untie me and fuck me."

He smiled and stood, licking his fingers clean. Walking around the desk, he leaned close.

"Untie you? Fuck you?" he asked, giving a throaty laugh.

"Untie me. Fuck me." I repeated, this time leaning forward, kissing him. I thrust my tongue into his mouth, tasting myself and moaning. I tangled my tongue with his before biting his lip – hard.

Hugh gasped, leaning, back and touching his lip. A dark look crossed his face as he looked down at me.

"Oh." The word was hollow as it left his lips.

A small voice in the back of my head whispered, *you done fucked up.*

A humorless smile curved Hugh's lips. It was clear how precarious my position was.

Immediately, I started to backpedal.

"Wait. W-wait." I wasn't sure what to say.

"I'm afraid you're all out of freebies, Denise." He sounded disappointed, but the fact that he was rock hard said otherwise. Hugh caught my glance down and laughed again. "First, let's address your requests. Untie you?" he chuckled. "No. Fuck you? Oh, absolutely not."

Hugh reached down out of sight for a moment before he popped back up. His hands went to my bra, caressing the fabric before a pair of scissors came into view and cut through the fabric, freeing my breasts.

"Oh. Muthafucka!" I said before I could stop myself. I'm all for fun and games, but I loved that bra.

Hugh watched me, contemplating. After a few moments, his thumb traced my lip.

"Second, remind me: what are your safe words?"

I hesitated. This was unfamiliar territory. I wanted this, more than I could even begin to make sense of, but this was an out. A way to enjoy him and what he had to offer, find the passion between us in a way I was used to. But that wasn't the Denise that walked into this room. This Denny was all about thrill and feeling wanted. And what I wanted was to surrender.

That Denny replied, "Grapefruit for slow, habanero for stop."

"And what did we say about bad girls, Denise?" he asked, his tone overly patient.

"They get punished," I replied, squirming, knowing that I couldn't get away.

"Right. Now, would you say that you're being a bad girl, Denise?"

He was clearly torturing me, drawing out the anticipation of whatever he had planned, and I was at his mercy.

"Maybe?" I replied, watching as his smile disappeared. He stared at me, while his touch on my mouth remained gentle. After a few seconds, I couldn't help but fill the silence. "Yes."

"Yes." He agreed, his fingers moving down my chest, circling my nipple. "And bad girls get?"

My stomach somersaulted.

"Punished."

Hugh gripped my nipple tight between two fingers and twisted, slowly. I jerked against him as the pain increased and gritted my teeth.

When he let go, a rush of endorphins flooded through me. I moaned and squirmed while Hugh stood back, watching me writhe in front of him.

His mouth grabbed the nipple he had just freed, his tongue lapping gently at its peak. His fingers grabbed my other nipple and repeated the same slow, painful twist.

This time he bit and pulled the nipple he'd so lovingly caressed. I cried out, shutting my eyes and focused on breathing through the pain.

When he switched breasts, I tried to squirm away, but he only quickened his twists. The heady mix of pain and pleasure was unbearable. I squeezed my thighs together, feeling the juices dripping as I struggled to move away.

Again and again, he took turns twisting and licking until I was delirious. His teeth bit down and instead of continuing his torture on my other breast, his hand trailed down my body and found my clit.

I was so close I jerked my hips against his hands, rabid with the need to cum, needing it like I needed breath. It was just there, just out of reach, I rotated my hips in Hugh's rhythm, feeling it teetering on the edge.

Hugh's hand and mouth went away, and I wailed in despair. A shuddering breath caught in my chest. I was frustrated.

Grapefruit, habanero, hell, all of the fruits and vegetables were on the tip of my tongue, but I bit my cheek and took deep breaths.

"Denny." I ignored him, my eyes squeezed tight, trying to calm down the rage of hormones and emotions running rampant.

"Denise, look at me." He was using that tone, and I knew if I didn't do what he said, the torture would continue. I couldn't take much more, so I swallowed my frustration and opened my eyes.

Hugh's smug face was inches from my face.

"That's it. You cum when I say you do."

His fingers lightly skimmed my thigh and I jumped.

"Repeat it."

I grunted as he teased closer and closer to my throbbing pussy, staying just far enough away that the ache was almost painful. He raised his eyebrows as his hand hovered over my mound.

"I cum when you say I do," I growled.

He leaned in and kissed me. It was all teeth and tongue, forcing me to duel with him. I felt his hand continue its teasing assault, this time it was his palm circling around and around as I tilted my hips beneath him.

Fingers probed my entrance and I whimpered against his mouth.

"Shh," he said, pushing his fingers into me slowly, leaning back and watching me intently as he curled his fingers upward and explored until he found the spot that made me cry out.

"There it is." His tone was triumphant, like he'd unlocked some secret cheat code. As he started to caress that spot over and over, I realized he had. The movements against my g spot started slowly, in a teasing, tight circle. My pussy milked his fingers as he worked to keep the same torturous pace.

I was on fire. Grabbing at the ties, my legs began to shake as the heat consumed me.

"Please, don't stop," the plea came from my chest, a begging grunt in a voice I'd never used before.

His fingers started to move a little quicker, the circles a little broader.

My grunt became a long moan, I wanted to move, but I was afraid to lose it. Afraid he wouldn't let me cum, so I kept my hips as still as I could, feeling my legs shake harder.

I was putty in his hands, and he drove me to the edge. Tears welled in my eyes as I started to murmur something, anything. He couldn't stop. Not now. Not when I was so close.

"Please, please let me cum," I mewled.

"That's it, that's my good girl. Cum."

I stumbled over the edge. Everything around me became fuzzy and I went numb. I was so overcome by it that it felt like my heart had stopped beating in my chest, my entire body shaking as I felt liquid gushing across the desk.

My throat was raw as I cried out over and over, clenching as my orgasm built and built with every twist of his fingers.

Even as he pulled free, my muscles contracted, and I kept coming, feeling the waves cresting over and over.

It wasn't until Hugh gathered me in his arms that I realized my hands were free. He leaned over me, entering me in one glorious thrust. I clung to him with my thighs as he grunted, his hips staying still while my muscles continued to contract.

"Oh my God," he choked out.

I was hungry for more, I was craving him. Reaching for him, I pulled his hips in close. Hugh swore and dropped his head back. He was sweating and struggling to stay still. But I didn't want him still – I wanted to feel every inch of him pumping into me, touching all of my spots and sending me into the stratosphere.

I rolled my hips beneath him, smiling. Hugh grabbed my throat and pushed me back down on the desk, hovering over me.

"You're a menace. I wanted to take my time," he said, pulling his dick in and out at an achingly slow rhythm.

I laughed, tilting my hips so he could seat himself deeper in me.

"I think you should take what you want," I repeated.

Hugh reached for my hand at his waist, and he slid our fingers to my clit, moving with me, building me back up.

"I'll take it, alright," he whispered.

He grabbed at my thighs and pulled almost all the way out before slamming back into me.

"That's good. Holy shit," I said, my fingers swirling around my clit.

I felt like I was dying of thirst, and every pump of his dick was giving me the hydration I craved.

The pace became more frantic. What was methodical was becoming hurried and rough. He pinned my thighs back as our bodies slammed together, his grunts becoming wild. I was moaning with him, complimenting his every stroke inside me. Every touch brought me closer to the precipice. His dick was the perfect fit, he was the perfect fit, and I was rabid with need.

"Yes, harder," I said.

It was like he was waiting for me. He sat me up.

"Turn over."

I slipped off the edge of the desk and had barely bent over before he grabbed my waist and started fucking me from behind. I cried out over and over as his pace became relentless, and the office was filled with the sound of our bodies meeting.

Every cell in my body was attuned to this moment, to soaking up all of what he was bringing to life in me.

My fingers moved back to my clit, but I didn't need to because I was already there. The orgasm roared to life, turning my legs to jelly, and Hugh cried out behind me over and over as he slowed his strokes. His forehead rested on my back as we both breathed heavily, trying to get our bearings.

I shuddered, clenching again and again with a mind entirely her own.

"Ah, ah, don't start something you can't finish," Hugh said, still inside me.

His hands swept across my sides, massaging my sweaty skin. He made no hurry to move, and I was glad for it. His weight pressing down on me was delicious as we both caught our breath.

If I was boneless earlier, I was utterly ravaged now. Hugh slowly lifted his hips, pulling free of my sensitive pussy with a wet plop. I made a noise of protest at the sensation as Hugh leaned forward again, placing all of his weight back on me.

Laying there, I felt the rise and fall of his chest, the slickness of his skin against mine, and the thundering of my heart in my chest. It all equaled something I hadn't felt in a long time: utter satisfaction.

Hugh kissed my back, his tongue tracing my skin.

"You are – magnificent," he said, lightly nipping my skin.

"That was definitely a joint effort." I laughed. "I don't think I'm ever going to look at your desk the same."

His hands moved down to massaging my ass, and I let out a sigh of bliss.

"Good." Hugh's tone was arrogant, and I couldn't even be mad at it. The way he'd had me shaking and shivering, he'd earned the right.

"Who knew you had a little freak in you," I whispered.

"Denise, the things I want to do to you. You're never going to be the same."

As Hugh grabbed a handful of ass and jiggled, I didn't doubt that for a second.

It was too late for BART, not that I'd have taken BART home at this hour anyway.

I'd pulled myself together and called for a ride, my body boneless. My mind was racing, but thankfully I'd already programmed a stop into my ride home. The car pulled alongside the pharmacy, and I hopped out.

"I'll be quick," I said to the driver.

Gathering my dress, I held it up off the ground as I speed-walked into the store. My hope was that no one would notice I was braless. My sneakers squeaked against the floor as I charged through the aisles.

I headed for the section that housed the condoms, shaking my head as I walked past them. The copious amount of fucking I'd just engaged in should have used one, but here I was, buying a morning-after pill at four a.m. like I was some carefree twenty-something.

There were a few options to choose from, but I grabbed the name brand I recognized and walked back towards the register. It was super dead, unsurprisingly, and I was able to drop the box right on the cashier's counter. The shelf behind him was covered in top-shelf booze. I paused, a hilarious thought in my brain.

I leaned forward, watching the cashier's eyes glance down at my tits swaying under my dress. Dude looked twenty, so I didn't bother to check him. It wasn't worth it.

"What kind of whiskey you got back there?"

"What are you looking for?" The man was speaking straight to my tits like they were going to answer him.

"My boyfriend just got out of prison. He likes the expensive stuff. You know how it is." I gave a loud laugh.

The cashier immediately looked away and turned towards the liquor.

"We have Macallan, but the highest we go is 12 years, you could also do Blanton's which, frankly, we shouldn't even have," he said, pulling two bottles down for me to see.

"Macallan I've heard of but Blanton's?" I asked, eyeing both bottles.

"Super high quality. Single barrel. It's what the enthusiasts drink."

"Perfect. I'm sold. I'll take it. Oh, and a water too," I said, snagging water from the display.

Popping open the box, I nudged the pill out of the foil and downed it.

The cashier had gone from interested to slightly terrified, and I just smiled at him.

I bopped my card on the machine before he could read off the total and smiled sweetly.

"Do you have a trash can?" I asked, handing him the box.

He took it as I grabbed the bottle and walked back to my Uber. I drank a bit more water watching the city go by, and I smiled, feeling my sore pussy twinge underneath me.

By the time Monday morning rolled around, I was a nervous, hot mess.

I'd spent an abnormally long time in my closet that morning, sifting through every outfit until I found the perfect one. And the whiskey? That was starting to feel desperate and not like a funny joke.

As I stood on BART, I was second-guessing everything. I was so in my head that I'd nearly missed my stop.

Stepping off the train just as the doors closed shut, I knew this needed to stop. I needed to get it together. It was a regular day, just like any other, and I couldn't walk into the office like this.

I pulled out my cell phone and rolled through my contacts and pressed 'Cleo'.

All it took was two rings. Cleo never let me down.

"It's seven in the morning. You better be dead or dying." Cleo was always one for the dramatics, but I knew the phrase that would get her attention.

"I have tea," I said, sitting down on a bench, staring at the escalators meant to take me to my doom.

I'd known Cleo since I was ten. Her parents moved to the city from bumfuck Utah.

"What did you do?" Cleo asked, her voice an octave lower than normal.

"You mean who?" I whispered, looking around like the morning commuters could see the giant scarlet A on my chest.

"You dirty bitch!" Cleo shrieked. I gave her a moment to calm down and after a second she cleared her throat and said, "Continue."

"We had our party on Friday – "

"Nah, nah, nah, we ain't starting at the beginning. Start at the end and go backward."

"Hugh," I said.

"Hugh? I thought – hold up, I'm putting you on speaker." I heard a little rustling and already knew she was internet stalking him. She gasped. "You never told me Hugh was fine! Den, you made him sound like some hip sixty-year-old who just happened to have some melanin. You're telling me you've been working beside this venti iced mocha latte for years and you only just now let him get in your guts? Tell me everything."

"First, gross. Second, it just kind of happened and then happened again. We made a deal that it's only for two nights–"

"God dammit!"

"Cleo."

"Sorry, I'll be quiet," she said, knowing damn well she wouldn't.

"He's a good friend."

"Was he a good fuck, too? I know I said I'd shut up. But was he?"

"Cleo. Cleeeo," I said, drawing out her name and sighing.

"That good? Damn," she muttered.

"How am I supposed to go into work and pretend like nothing has changed?"

There was silence on the other end for a moment while she pondered.

"Baby, you don't. You had your world rocked by this man, right? You just have to act accordingly. Keep it professional, pretend like you don't know what his dick looks like when your coworkers are around, and try and keep it out of the office."

"Too late. He had me speaking tongues tied to his desk," I whispered into the microphone.

"Tied to his desk!?" She cackled. I was sure she was also kicking her feet in the air. "Oh, you in danger, girl."

"I know, Whoopi," I moaned, my hand covering my face.

"Is this the wrong time to ask about the freeloader-sized elephant in the room?"

"Cleo. What am I doing?" I wailed. "It all made sense but–"

"Tell me how it made sense," Cleo demanded.

"I just, everything has been so weird. I got the promotion, but it doesn't feel any different. And I'm carrying it all on my back and I have been for so long, and I wanted to feel good and have fun. I did feel good. I did have fun. It was absolutely fucking glorious. I deserved to feel wanted and seen as Denise, a sexual being, not just a roommate and a wallet."

"That. That right there, Den. You needed something, and Hugh gave it to you in spades. You are worried about everything under the damn sun that could happen, but you need to focus on how you feel and what that man gave you. He made you feel seen and wanted." Cleo's tone changed. She was getting into her groove and giving me the energy and focus I needed.

"You are a strong and capable black woman. Now walk your ass into work like you own that place, take that paycheck you worked hard for, and try not to stare at that man's desk and have another orgasm."

I cackled and shook my head.

"You're right," I said.

"Bitch, I'm always right. Now go make my money. Dinner is on you on Thursday. Don't try to cancel on me, either. I'll show up at your job and start flirting with your new dick."

"Cleo!" I said in faux outrage.

"Denise!" She said, mocking me.

"Thank you," I said. "I needed that."

"Kisses. Text me. I'm now living vicariously through you, so I have to know everything," Cleo laughed as she hung up.

If there was one thing I was going to feel after a conversation with Cleo, it was clarity. She'd known me for so long. She saw right through my bullshit and gave it to me straight. I'd been putting off our plans for a month. I didn't doubt for a second that she'd show up at my office if I told her I had to work late again.

I waded through the crowd towards the escalator and hugged the whiskey close to me.

I'd known Hugh for years. Things didn't have to be weird. Hell, I brought him stuff to work all the time. Mainly it was my mama's collard greens or a piece of pecan pie, but still. I think that counted.

It was cold as shit, but it usually was this time of morning. I practically ran from the escalator into the building entrance, thanking the genius that made the financial district so walkable.

Bill wasn't at the guard desk, thank goodness. I didn't need that man giving me the eyes and the eyebrows before going upstairs to face the music.

Within five minutes, I was walking through Foxx. The floor was quiet as it normally was this early in the morning and I loved it. It was my calm before the storm, and it gave me the space to think. I gave a half-wave to the only person in their cubby, and they waved back.

When I entered my office, I saw the heels from Friday were sitting right where I left them. I ignored them, dropping my briefcase on the desk and shrugging off my coat. Opening my briefcase, I grabbed my black mesh Manolo pumps and kicked off my transit shoes to slide them on. I looked down at my outfit one last time.

The robin egg blue midi dress had a faux wrap skirt that swished when I moved. I tugged at the bottom to get it back to the right place, smoothing my waist. It was professional, but the side slit was a tad more risqué than I would have normally chosen.

I eyed the bottle. *Suck it up,* I said to myself, grabbing it and walking out of my office.

Hugh's back was to me when I walked in. I stood in the doorway for a moment, taking him in. He was bent over his filing cabinet, his charcoal suit pants fitted to a juicy and round booty. It took a lot not to make a comment, I silently walked in and placed the whiskey on his desk with a clunk.

"Good morning, Denise."

Hugh flashed me a smile while sitting back down at his desk.

"Hugh." I sat across from him stiffly and watched him eye the paper bag. My gaze stayed on Hugh's face. I refused to look at his desk, or his arms, or think about the gloriously talented fingers that were folded in front of him.

"How was your weekend?" he asked as he leaned back in his chair.

I mimicked him nervously, leaning back in my chair as well.

"Relaxing. Yours?"

"Enlightening." He paused, motioning towards the bag. "What's this?"

I couldn't read him. But I'd already come this far…

Digging into the bag, I pulled out the whiskey and placed it in front of him.

"I think you ran out. Maybe I'll get a glass this time." I tapped the horse and jockey atop the bottle.

Hugh blinked and turned the bottle to see the label, a sinister smile creeping across his lips.

"Denny, we both know why you didn't get a drop of my whiskey."

A little thrill ran through me at his words. His tone was laden with words unsaid.

"Do we?" I relaxed, recognizing the game for what it was. Leaning back again, I crossed my leg over my thigh. Hugh glanced down at my now-visible thighs, his gaze hungry. Now I had his attention.

He cleared his throat and straightened his tie. I followed his movements, realizing it was the same tie that had been tied tightly to my wrist forty-eight hours ago. Before I could stop them, my eyes glanced to the edge of his desk, where my bare ass and pussy had been at his mercy. A flush crept up my neck as I tightened my thighs.

Hugh's smile grew wider, he knew he was getting to me.

"I could be convinced to share. But there would be criteria."

"Oh? Do tell." I replied, ignoring the fact that we both knew I was way more flustered than he was.

"One could say that whiskey is reserved for those who behave," Hugh spoke softer, and I felt the butterflies come back, colliding with desire in my stomach.

I grabbed the whiskey and stood, walking around the desk. Hugh's eyebrow shot up, and his gaze fell to my fingers running along the side of the desk I was bent over as I came again and again.

Hugh growled as I leaned over him to put the whiskey in his cabinet. I made sure to run my hand along his thigh as I moved. Leaning back, I saw he was already hard as a rock. I gave it a little pat, and it leapt against my palm.

Hugh's mouth dropped open as I stood.

"I guess we'll see," I said with a shrug, walking out of his office. I turned around just enough to see his eyes narrow and watch my ass as I walked out the door.

My cheeks hurt from how wide my smile was. Cleo was right. Hugh made me feel alive. All the other shit I could figure out later, but right now – at this moment – there was a gorgeous man who made me turn into a puddle with a glance. And that was what I needed.

I walked around my desk to plop into my chair when I saw it. The bag was neatly tucked away out of view. Confused, I grabbed it and peeked inside.

An exact duplicate of my metallic blue bra was hiding beneath some tissue paper. I double-checked the tag for the size and let out an astonished chuckle. Below it sat two more long-lined balconettes, one in a deep, silky red and the other sheer black. Matching panties were folded neatly at the bottom.

A note was tucked into the side that read: when I break it, I buy it.

I ran my fingers along the silk and let out a breath. Gently placing it back in the bag, I slid it back under my desk and my hand went to my mouth. I was shook.

One thing for certain and two things for sure: I was in trouble, and I wasn't going to be the same when this was done.

Denise and Hugh will return.

ABOUT THE AUTHOR

Thank you for diving into Ayla Cox's world for a little while.

When Ayla's not on her knees in a fit of passion and lust, she's devouring any book she can get her hands on.

On the off chance that Ayla has time off, you may find her frolicking on a beach or hiding away in a lake cabin, recharging her batteries, both figuratively and literally.

If you love what you've read, give her a follow and leave a few encouraging words.

Ayla Cox can be found on [TikTok @AylaCoxWrites](#).

STILL HERE?
You'll see Hugh and Denise again, I promise!

Printed in Great Britain
by Amazon